This book belongs to:

✗ _____

# HAMMIE'S HELP SQUAD

# F&D Publishing

Hammie's Help Squad
By Mary F. Block and Denise J. Snider
Published by F&D Publishing

ISBN 979-8-9857999-0-3

*This book is dedicated to those unwavering*
*friends in our small circle:*

Craig Renwick — for your generosity and enthusiasm

Ken Bloom —for your expertise and guidance

Roger E. — for the "character"

Hammie's story is one of kindness, acceptance and generosity. It is a sweet tale of unusual friendships and commitment to helping others, without reservation.

We hope that children everywhere will understand and use these ideas as they grow.

# Can you find all of these items on each page?

 Hammie loves his ball!

 He loves to chew on his bone!

 Can you spot Roger? He may be hiding!

 Where is the red leaf?

Hammie's house is next to a large oak tree on the edge of a beautiful forest. He shares his tree with a peculiar and funny old owl named Roger.

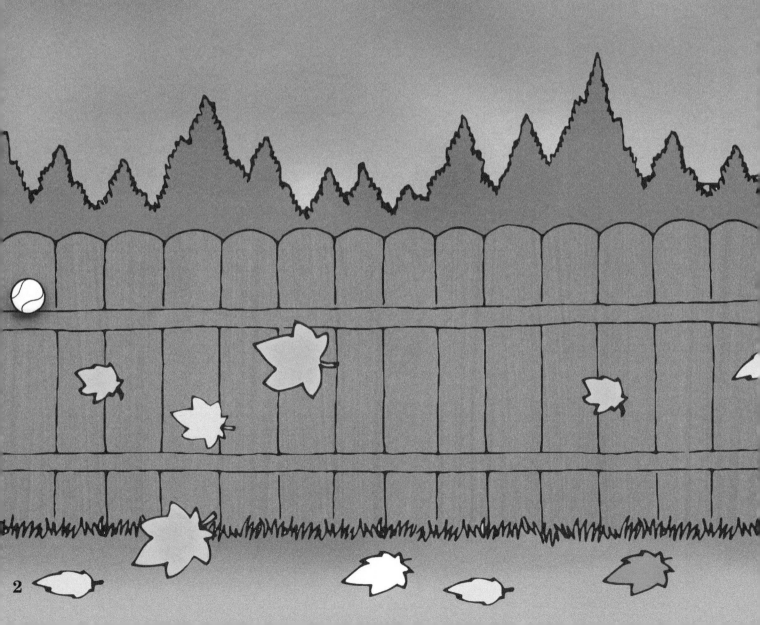

2

3

Their adventure started out one cold and stormy morning. Hammie loves this kind of weather…lots of wind, dark clouds and piles of wet leaves to walk through — just like his homeland in Scotland.

Hammie picked out one of his favorite bow-ties and a sweater and dressed himself to go for his 'walkie'. Hammie's owners made him a special door in the big fence that leads into the woods so he can come and go when he likes.

7

Halfway down the path through the woods behind his house, Roger started flapping his wings like crazy and Hammie stopped, sniffed and smelled danger!!!

His ears shot straight up and he stopped in his tracks as he saw the beautiful lady BlueJay, sitting along the side of the road, crying.

"Please help me", she cried, "please, it's my husband who's fallen from the big maple tree"!

Hammie ran over and there, in a large pile of branches and leaves, he found a kind of unusual looking bird, his glasses all tangled and one wing slightly bent from the fall.

Together, Hammie, Roger and the lady BlueJay
freed him and they sat and introduced themselves.
Hammie learned that Mr. Woody Bird and Mrs.
Marion Berry Bird are homeless—their tree-home
was blown down in the storm.

They became instant friends! He invited them to move into a nice house set into the upper branches of his tree and told them they would have a forever-home there. They would become Hammie's new family.

They were so happy to have found each other that
they vowed to come to the aid of any and all animals
that needed their help.

Right there in the forest, they formed

# HAMMIE'S HELP SQUAD

23

## ABOUT FRAN

A native of Southern California, I enjoyed a very interesting career in
the music industry. I am now happily retired and living in Northern California
with my sister and co-author, Denise. We are joyfully surrounded by family,
lots of great kids and animals. The time I have spent reading and interacting
with nieces, nephews and my great-grandchildren are precious memories and
have contributed to the idea for creating this book.

The inspiration for the book came from my ever-curious and sweet tempered
Scottie dog, Hammie. Hopefully, it is the first in many more adventures that
parents and children will enjoy together.

## ABOUT DENISE

Originally from Southern California, now living in Northern California.
Worked for 25 years as a private investigator. Mother of two, grandmother of
four, I spent many wonderful hours reading to grandkids.

Hammie's Help Squad is a collaboration with my sister, Fran, and it has been
a true labor of love to see it become a great adventure we hope all kids and
parents will enjoy.

*Whatever you can do (or dream you can),
begin it.*

*Boldness has genius, power and magic in it.*

—JOHANN WOLFGANG VON GOETHE

9 798985 799903